Mara's Stories

GLIMMERS IN THE DARKNESS

Gary Schmidt

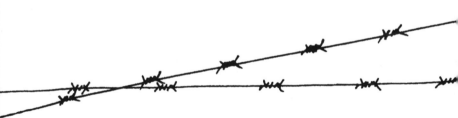

HENRY HOLT AND COMPANY SQUARE FISH

SQUARE
FISH

An Imprint of Macmillan

MARA'S STORIES. Copyright © 2001 by Gary Schmidt. All rights reserved.
Printed in the United States of America by R. R. Donnelley & Sons
Company, Harrisonburg, Virginia. For information, address
Square Fish, 175 Fifth Avenue, New York, N.Y. 10010.

Square Fish and the Square Fish logo are trademarks of Macmillan
and are used by Henry Holt and Company under license from Macmillan.

Library of Congress Cataloging-in-Publication Data
Schmidt, Gary D. Mara's stories / by Gary Schmidt.   p.   cm.
Includes bibliographical references. Summary: Each evening, in one of the barracks
of a Nazi death camp, a woman shares stories that push back the darkness,
cold, and fear, bringing hope to the women and children who listen.
1. Holocaust, Jewish (1939–1945)—Juvenile fiction. [1. Holocaust, Jewish
(1939–1945)—Fiction. 2. Jews—Fiction. 3. Storytelling—Fiction. 4. Concentration
camps—Fiction.] I. Title. PZ7.S3527 Mar 2001 [Fic]—dc21   2001016969

ISBN 978-0-312-37388-7
Originally published in the United States by Henry Holt and Company
First Square Fish Edition: 2008
Designed by Donna Mark
Square Fish logo designed by Filomena Tuosto
10 9 8 7 6 5 4
mackids.com

The prayer "The Ancestors" in the story "The Reply" and the prayer "The Priestly Blessing" in
the story "The Pretzel Bakers" are excerpted from *My People's Prayer Book: Traditional Prayers,
Modern Commentaries, Vol. 2: The Amidah* © 1998 by Rabbi Lawrence A. Hoffman (Woodstock, Vt.: Jewish Lights Publishing). The prayer "The Section on Tassels" in the story "The
Promise of the *Talis Koten*" is from *My People's Prayer Book: Traditional Prayers, Modern Commentaries, Vol. 1: The Shma and Its Blessings* © 1997 by Rabbi Lawrence A. Hoffman (Woodstock, Vt.: Jewish Lights Publishing). Order by mail or call (800) 962-4544 or online at
www.jewishlights.com. Permission granted by Jewish Lights Publishing, P.O. Box 237, Woodstock, Vt. 05091.

For Malvin and Millie Vitriol
and for
Howard and Libbijane Goldman,
for the stories—of which you are so much a part—
that fill my
childhood years

Contents

Author's Note

There are many ways at coming at a truth. But when one turns to the Holocaust, there is one Truth at the core: that six million people—one million of them children—were murdered because they were Jewish. In the most bloody century of human history, the Holocaust stands as the most horrific testament to human evil and darkness.

The stories that my Mara tells in the darkness of the concentration-camp barracks are a mix of tales. Some are tales that she heard from her father the Rabbi, but she has taken those Hasidic tales and brought them into her own time—as will any good storyteller. She finds that their truths are just as present in the barracks of the Holocaust as they were in early-nineteenth-century Poland or Russia, that these truths become even more powerful when brought into those barracks. But she also tells folktales that have grown up in the camps, told from one prisoner to another, hammered out in the forge of common suffering by an entire people.

Mara is my character, my narrator. Her name means "bitter" in Hebrew, and I have given her that name not because she herself is bitter, but because she lives in the bitterest of times. I hope that she may, in some small measure, stand for all the men and women of the barracks who tried, in the middle of the darkest night, to bring some light to themselves and to their children—through making rag toys, through cheering words, through pictures, through the comfort of touch, and through stories.

What is most remarkable about all of Mara's stories is their testimony not to despair—though she has every reason to despair—but instead to light and warmth and hope and life. The stories celebrate all that is good and strong in the human spirit, all that cannot be destroyed by evil. It is one of the reasons why the stories are powerful for all listeners, all readers, and why the stories are still alive today. They are stories, as writer and folklorist Ellen Frankel has said, on their way to becoming legends. They come, like the tales of the Baal Shem Tov, as stories for us all, in every generation, always new, always true.

Gary Schmidt

Stories in the Darkness

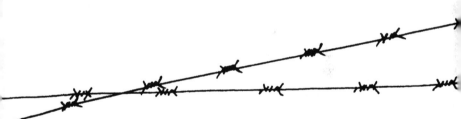

*N*ight.

It always seems to be night in the camps—or at least it always seems to be dark.

Somewhere the sun must come up every morning. Somewhere there is more than only dust and clouds and ashes. There must be some place, there must be some place that is warm and bright and green.

But not here. Not in this death camp. Not here.

Here is always cold. Here is always fear and pain. Here is always hunger. Here is always waiting for . . . for what?

Night.

But there is one moment every day in one of the barracks when the dark and the cold seem to pull away and be forgotten. It is in Mara's barracks, which is a barracks just like any other except that this one holds Mara. At night, hungry and trying not to look at the empty places where friends slept just a night or two before, the women come back and gather their children around them. They hold them and share their food. They smile to hide their soul terror.

4

And then they come to Mara's bunk.

Mara is waiting for them all. No matter what new wound bleeds through her shirt, she is waiting. No matter what new bruise is swelling, she is waiting. She is waiting with the light and the warmth of stories. Everyone gathers around, and from her lips to their ears the stories go, and for a little while the camp disappears, and for a little while they are all free.

Each evening it is the same. Mara reaches out and takes a child onto her lap—a different little one each night. "When my father the Rabbi would sit us around him and tell a story," she begins, "he would ask God to listen as well. 'God,' he would say, 'make me a teller of stories, because all stories are Yours. And if You would lend me one now, I will tell it and then give it back to You.'" She lifts her hands to heaven when she speaks.

And everyone in the barracks is still, so still. And the story comes to Mara as though God Himself were giving it. Mara smiles. She nods. And then she tells it.

Many of the stories are of long ago, in the days of the great rabbis whose lives were lives of light. But in this barracks there is no long ago. There is only now. It seems as if there has always only been now. And so the tales even of long ago and far away become tales of now and here, as if they had just happened. As if they are happening even now.

Sometimes Mara's stories are sad, and the dark lines below her eyes darken, and the hollows of her cheeks fall even farther in. Sometimes the stories are too terrible to speak, and she tells them very softly, in a voice that is hardly a whisper, slivers of sound. Sometimes the stories are lonesome, and as she tells them, her eyes fill for those whom she misses, whom they all miss. And sometimes, sometimes the stories are funny, and Mara laughs out loud, and her cheeks hint at a long-lost glow.

Night after night, night after night the stories push back the darkness and the cold. Those who listen carry them through the next day, and often the thought of the next night's story is all that keeps the women from stepping across the dead-lines that rim the camp.

And the children?

The children listen. The children listen and understand.

The Violinist and the Master

In a camp in Poland, there was once a young violinist named Salek. He had been in the camp for two years, and in all that time he had never ceased practicing his music. He had no violin and he had no bow, but he practiced nonetheless. In the long hours of pain and boredom, he dangled his legs over the edge of the platform, held his chin just so and his hands out, and fingered through Schumann, and Brahms, and Mozart.

And he heard the music in the air. Even though no one else around him could hear it, he did.

Then one night, half of those in his barracks were marched away. Awakened from sleep, they were marched away and could take nothing with them.

That night, Salek played silently into the darkness, trying to fill it with music.

In the morning, a new group of souls was marched into the barracks, and rifle butts forced them four, five, six abreast onto the wooden slats that would be their bunks. And across from Salek on the upper platform, unbelievably, was the Master Violinist he had heard in Prague. It couldn't be, but it was. The Master.

With the shouting and the calling and the crying, Salek could not speak to him. Perhaps the Master would not have answered anyway. He looked as though he were at the rim of the Sheol.

Salek stared across at him. How often had he listened to this man's music! How often had his soul breathed on every tone that shimmered, or danced, or thundered, or struck from his strings! Salek knew that in his best moments, in his very best moments, he could never make the music that this Master made. But the knowledge had not brought despair to him, only wonder at the gifts of God. That God had touched this man so that he could make music—no, not make—*breathe* music like the living breath of God! Salek shook his head at the thought.

The next night, Salek sat on the edge of his platform and called across. "Master!" He had to whisper so that the *kapos* outside would not hear him. But the Master did not stir. "Master," Salek called again. "Master!"

Nothing.

Salek dared not risk any more calls.

The next night, he tried again, but the head of the Master was drooped even lower than it had been the first night. "Master!" Salek called. The Master did not answer.

The third night, Salek did not call. He dangled his legs over the edge of the platform, held his chin just so and his hands out. And he began to play. With his bow of air he drew through a long and trembling *adagio* from Schumann, then spurted to a quick *rondo* from Brahms. His eyes closed with the beauty of the music. And when he opened them again, finishing with a short, quick *presto* from Mozart, the Master was looking at him.

He had heard. He had heard the music.

The next night, the Master and Salek sat across from each other. They dangled their legs over the edge of the platform, held their chins just so and their hands out, and played a Corelli duet. The Master tapped the air with his foot for the rhythm, and Salek took the second line. The music from the two of them interlaced like two rosy vines until they reached a perfect bloom of a note that they held and held—a little longer than Corelli might have wished, but neither Salek nor the Master wanted the duet to end.

And those around them heard. They heard the music too.

After that night, and for many, many nights afterward, the Master and Salek played the Corelli duet, their bows waving in thin air, just thin air. But the music that came from that air! All those in the barracks held their breath with the astonishment of it. They all closed their eyes to the wonder of it. Their hearts forgot to beat with the joy of it.

And always Salek heard the Master's line louder and sweeter, the line of a musician touched by God.

One night, the guards burst into the barracks, bristling with flashlights and bayoneted rifles. The glare their lights threw down on the prisoners was like the glare of hell. One by one the guards called the numbers, and the prisoners looked at their tattooed arms to see if theirs was the one called. The barracks filled with silent weeping, as the dreadful march of numbers drummed on and on.

And when the last number was called, Salek looked across at the Master and saw that it was his. It was his.

With a sigh, the Master looked to heaven and then began to climb down from his platform. But Salek was quicker. He slid down first and stood beneath the Master, looking at the hands that had held themselves just so to make such music.

"Stay," he whispered. "Stay for the music. Stay for its joy."

The Master's eyes widened, but he shook his head.

"Hold him," said Salek, and though the Master struggled, hands grabbed him and pinned him to his bunk. Salek walked out of the barracks and into the cold night, his soul rising to heaven—if not higher.

. . .

Someday, the camp will be liberated. And the Master will survive.

He will live for many years afterward, and give many concerts. His music will breathe joy. His music will speak of hope and love and spring and summer, of children and home and peace—of all the good and joyful things in this old and tired world.

And in all his concerts, he will end by playing a single line from the Corelli duet, a single lonely line that nevertheless will thrill with the sounds of happiness. And he will always weep, my children. He will always weep.

From joy, his audiences will think. From joy.

Fear and Faith
in a Bloodied Earth

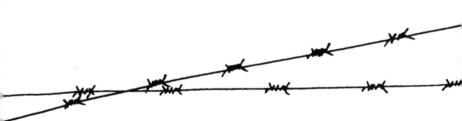

It happens on some nights that Mara remembers her home, and though the days when she was a girl seem as if they must be part of another lifetime, she closes her eyes and suddenly is at the seder table. Its silver lamp, lit with seven white candlesticks, glows on the tablecloth that her mother has pressed to a linen crispness. She smells red wine, cinnamon, sweet wax, and the slightly bookish scent of the Rabbi, her father. He stands and begins the prayers—she can hear them still—and Mara feels the Divine Presence softly brush a hand across her cheek.

Afterward she sits by her father, and he tells her stories of the great Hasidim and their wonderful doings. Stories of the mysteries they understood, of the miracles they held in the palms of their hands, of the awful heavenly burdens that turned their feet to dancing and their lips to song.

On such nights, as the stories of the Hasidim fill her, Mara tells stories about the years before the camps, and of those who escaped—and those who did not.

The Dark of the Earth

Many, many years ago, it happened that Zusia and Elimelekh, two brother rabbis who had lived poor and bitter lives in exile, decided to come back to Poland to spread the mysteries of the Hasidim. For three years, no one had heard from them; some even thought that they might have died. So when Zusia and Elimelekh returned, their family and neighbors rejoiced.

But they were not what they had been.

Zusia brought with him God's glorious ecstasy, and those who saw him marveled at the terrible love he showed. Elimelekh brought with him God's fearful sadness, and those who saw him marveled at the holy grief he inspired. They walked from town to town, spreading the love and grief of God. And wherever they came, they left behind them a town that was forever changed. Forever closer to God.

One night, they arrived in a small village a day's walk from Kraków. Though it was cold, the long streaks of yellow light thrown onto the road from the windows made the town look warm. When they came to the center of the village, they looked up and down the road. Since no one knew that they were coming, no one was out to greet them, and Zusia and Elimelekh decided that they would find a poor house to stay in.

It was like so many villages where they had stayed before: A row of houses, some shabby, some straight and well lit against the night. A row of front yards hemmed with rough fences beside the main road, some leaning crazily and held up by only a worn rope. They heard the lowing of a cow, a late milker, and the last cackling of some geese just settling down. A goat complained about her lot. It was all the same.

And yet it was not all the same.

A deep darkness in the earth clung at their feet as they walked. They could feel it pulling at their boots, as though it had seeped into the ground like blood and now waited, a living sodden death. In the gathering darkness of night, they could almost smell it.

The brothers left. Quickly, silently, without saying anything to each other or to anyone else in the village, they left. They did not even pray the prayer of blessing.

At the crossroads, they passed the rough plank that announced the town's name: Oświęcim. In the German: Auschwitz.

A Globe

In the days when it was becoming impossible for a Jew to live as a Jew in Germany, Rabbi Weizmann took his son, Chaim, his only son, and together they walked hand-in-hand to the Ministry of Travel in Berlin. They waited for most of a day on a line that never seemed to move. But Chaim was patient and waited quietly. He knew that his father was nervous, and he did not want to upset him with even the smallest fidgeting.

When they finally reached the window of the clerk, he stared above their heads and yawned. He turned a small globe on the counter with his fingers. "Yes?" he asked. He looked at his watch.

"Sir," said Reb Weizmann, "my son and I are here to request passports. We would like to travel to Chicago, America."

"America is not taking Jews," said the clerk, and yawned again.

Reb Weizmann was stunned. "What does this mean, 'America is not taking Jews'?"

"It means that America is not taking Jews. You cannot go to Chicago, America. You cannot go to New York, America. You cannot go to anywhere, America."

"Then we will go to Paris, France."

The clerk shook his head. "France is not taking Jews."

"Rome, Italy?"

"Italy is not taking Jews."

"Portugal?"

The clerk shook his head again.

Behind him, Reb Weizmann could feel those waiting in line growing restless. He reached out to the clerk's spinning globe and stopped it with a finger. "Are they taking Jews here?" he asked, pointing to a country.

"No."

"Then here? Or here? Or here?"

But the clerk only shook his head.

As Chaim looked up, he saw a tear form in his father's eye and his father's face begin to tremble. Slowly, slowly Chaim reached out and took his father's hand. He held it tight, then turned to the clerk.

"Please, sir," said Chaim, "you should have another globe?"

The Spilled Soup

Once in the town of Lizensk, the Rabbi sat down with his disciples for the sabbath meal. Except for the Rabbi, they were all terribly fearful of the new laws that had been announced in their district. There would be new taxes upon them, greater by far than any they had yet seen. They could not go to a movie theater or to the public library. Their children could not go to the state school. They could not appear on the beaches or at the resorts— and even had they wished to appear, they could not go there, since they were not allowed on the trains or buses.

But now there was word of a new law that would be the most terrible yet. And no one knew what it might be.

So the disciples gathered and waited to hear what new part of their lives would be destroyed.

Slowly the Rabbi began to fill a bowl of soup for Mendel, the first disciple. Mendel watched him carefully, and when the Rabbi spilled some on the table, Mendel quickly wiped it up. He looked fearfully at his master, but the Rabbi did not look at him. He filled the second bowl, and again spilled some of the soup. And so with the third and the fourth. The disciples watched in wonder as he spilled some from each of the bowls in turn. Mendel's eyes were wide.

Finally the Rabbi filled his own bowl, and with a start, he tipped it over. All the soup spilled upon the table and dripped to the floor.

"Rabbi!" shouted Mendel. "What are you doing? You will have us all arrested!"

The other disciples looked at Mendel in astonishment. "Arrested?" they asked each other. "Arrested for spilling soup?"

But the Rabbi only smiled. "Do not worry," he said to Mendel. "Now for a time we are safe."

At that moment, in faraway Berlin, Adolf Hitler pushed aside some papers in disgust. Time and time again he had tried to sign them, but a breeze had wafted them to the floor, or a telephone call had interrupted, or a dog had barked, or an aide had called. And now he had spilled ink all over the new edict. He swore loudly. The edict would have to wait.

And so, because of the Rabbi's spilled soup, the Jewish families in Lizensk were safe for a little longer.

Voices Rising like Light

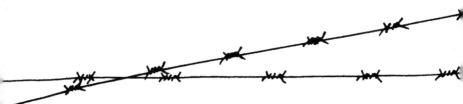

Each night, the women who return to the barracks are safe for a little longer. They have survived, and their children have survived. And when they gather around Mara to hear her stories, they know that they are still alive, and believe that they will be alive come morning.

When the stories end and they breathe again, the women rise silently and carry their children to their bunks. They lie down with them, some with blankets, many with none. They sleep.

And Mara watches them. She watches them all. And as she watches, she prays:

> *Blessed be the Lord in the light of day,*
>   *Blessed be the Lord in the dark of night.*
> *Blessed be the Lord when we wake,*
>   *Blessed be the Lord when we sleep.*
> *Blessed be the God of Israel, who does not slumber.*

And as she prays, she trembles. Could it not be true? After all, could it not be true?

But she knows that there will be a new story tomorrow, and her heart beats all the faster for it.

The Reply

The Rabbi stood by the eastern wall of his House of Prayer while it was being destroyed. First the windows had been shattered from the outside, and then the thrown bricks had become firebrands. The disciples who had fled inside for safety urged the Rabbi to run away with them, but he would not. "I will be with my people in their distress," he said, and then commanded his disciples to flee. And when they left, he stood all alone, silent, while the crowd with the firebrands surged in. The lurid light of the torches showed the rioters pulling down the chandeliers, hacking at the painted walls, tearing down the curtains from the lintel that had once guarded the Torah—gone long ago with the silver candlesticks.

The memory of reading that Torah by the light of those candlesticks! The Rabbi's eyes teared, and the rioters, believing that he wept only for his House of Prayer, jeered at him.

Blaring laughter as someone slashed the golden Hebrew letters that glowed over the lintel. They do not even know what they mean, thought the Rabbi. But he knew. He knew. "Know Before Whom You Stand."

Suddenly the crowd grew oddly quiet and then parted. His coat hanging loosely from his shoulders and his black gloves in the palm of his hand, a Nazi officer strode into the House of Prayer. He looked around him with a smile, then saw the Rabbi. His smile grew wider, and he walked to him slowly, with long, easy strides.

"So this is what you have come to," he said to the Rabbi.

The Rabbi did not answer.

"Do you see now, finally, how useless all this has been?" The officer waved an arm around him. "God is not here, or He would have stopped all this. Your prayers, your study, it is all rot. The scriptures that you hold so sacred, all rot."

"You would not say so, Captain, if you knew them."

The officer's smile grew even broader, and he leaned close. "But I do. I do know them. In my boyhood I heard them, and I knew that they were all rot. From the very first stories on. God in Eden, calling out to Adam 'Where are you?' If God is God, He would have known. Even a child can tell that it is all rot."

The Rabbi looked about at his ruined House of Prayer, where he would never worship again. Then he spoke quietly.

"Torah is eternal. It speaks to every person in every age. When God calls out to Adam 'Where are you?' He calls out to every person 'Where are you?' He means, 'How far have you come in this world?'" Now it was the Rabbi who leaned close, and he looked at the officer with piercing eyes. "So, Captain, how far have you come in this world, in all your forty-six years?"

The officer started and laid his hand against his heart. Then, quickly, he turned and left the House of Prayer, and the crowd followed him. None of them guessed that the Nazi officer was exactly forty-six years old.

Soon the Rabbi was alone, and it seemed to him as he began to pray that the light of the silver candlesticks filled that sanctuary.

Remember us for life, our king who delights in life, and write us in the book of life, for Your sake, our living God.

The Pretzel Bakers

When the Nazis crashed to power, everything in Germany became the fault of the Jews. Was there not enough money? The Jews hoarded it. Was there not enough bread? The Jews kept it for themselves. Were there not enough jobs? The Jews had them all.

Was the economy bad? Were there hard times? Was life not as good as it should be? Was Germany not as strong as it deserved to be?

The Jews. The Jews. Always the Jews.

One day, a quiet sabbath day, a Rabbi finished the prayers and blessings for his congregation: "Grant Your peace on Israel Your people and on Your heritage, and bless all of us as one. Blessed are You, Adonai, who brings peace." He waited as his people silently left the House of Prayer, and then he closed the doors to the Torah and turned to go. He was surprised to see a small boy waiting for him, smiling. Without a word, he took the hand that the boy held out to him, so small and so warm, and together they left the sanctuary.

But on the street, he found all his people waiting, looking up at him with frightened eyes. A sleek blue-black car hummed beside them on the road, and standing just by it was a Nazi officer.

In a smooth, slow movement, almost careless, the officer pulled a Luger from its holster and pointed it deliberately at the Rabbi. Smoothly, slowly, he came toward the Rabbi, who did not move. The only thing he seemed to sense was the movement of the officer coming like a snake toward him—and the small, warm hand still clasped in his own.

When the officer stood just a few feet from the Rabbi, he said, "Tell me, Jew, and tell me truly. Who is responsible for all the troubles of the Fatherland?" His words slithered, as smooth and slow as his steps.

The Rabbi looked down the length of the Luger; it seemed as if he could peer down the very barrel at the waiting bullet. Then he looked at all his people, watching him, some with their lips silently moving.

He turned back to the officer and said, quietly, "The Jews."

The officer smiled, and then laughed out loud. Slowly he put the Luger away.

And the boy's hand fell from the Rabbi's grasp. The Rabbi did not look down at him.

The officer smirked, then turned to go.

"And the pretzel bakers," said the Rabbi loudly.

The officer paused and looked back. Silence. Then, "Why the pretzel bakers?"

"Why the Jews?" answered the Rabbi, and felt again a warm, small hand grasp his own.

A Calf Is a Calf

Once upon a time, a farmer named Michael, having been taxed into almost complete poverty by the new laws, decided that he must sell one of the few animals he had left on his farm. His rooster was too old to bring any money, his cat too skinny, and his donkey too eager to kick, and so he decided to sell his calf. It was a fine white-and-red calf, and had the times been different Michael would have kept it for a milker. But nowadays he could never be sure of anything.

It happened that a Nazi officer came into the market that day to purchase nothing but mischief, and his eyes lit upon Michael and his calf. "How much do you want for that animal?" the officer asked.

Michael told him. "It is a fine calf, sir, and will serve you well."

"Calf?" said the officer, and turned to his aide beside him. "Did you hear that? He called that dog a calf!"

"It is a calf, sir."

"It is a dog, and a mongrel at that. But I have taken a fancy to it, and I will pay you a fair price for a mongrel."

"Then I will not sell it to you." At that, everyone in the market grew quiet, and the officer's eyes turned steely.

"Jew," he menaced quietly, "you will sell me that dog for a mongrel's price."

Well, what could Michael do? He sold the Nazi officer his calf for the price of a mongrel dog. And after the aide had handed over the pitifully few coins, the officer struck Michael to the ground. "Perhaps after this, you will remember that when an officer of the SS tells you an animal is a dog, it is a dog."

"I will remember," said Michael.

. . .

Some time later, the Nazi officer let it be known around town that he wished for a songbird to brighten his day. When the news came to Michael, he dusted his hair white with flour, put on an old coat, and pulled his cap low over his face. Then he took up his rooster and went to see the officer.

The officer handled papers on his desk. He hardly looked up. "What do you want?" he demanded.

"I have a songbird to sell to you."

The officer looked up. "Do you think I am blind? That is a rooster."

"It may look like a rooster, sir, but I assure you that it is a rare bird indeed, a bird that sings like the rising of the sun. No one else in the city has a songbird such as this. No one in Berlin itself has such a songbird."

The officer rubbed his hands with delight. "How much is the bird?"

"A songbird such as this, sir, comes at no cheap price." Michael named a figure that startled the officer, but he was so eager to have such a unique and rare bird—even if it did look like an old rooster—that he paid the sum. "You must be sure to place the bird near your bedside at nightfall," said Michael. And the officer took the bird and set it on a stand by his bedside.

The next morning, the rooster saw the sun pink the horizon, opened its wings to their full length, and began to screech out a hideous cawing from its old and grizzled throat. The officer put his hands over his ears, then his pillow over his ears, then his blanket over his ears, but nothing could stop the screeching. Finally he ran to his window and opened it wide. Then he grabbed the rooster and flung it out the window.

The rooster flapped to the ground, looked about, and then strutted down the road and back to the farm, where Michael was waiting to greet it happily.

· · ·

Some time later, the Nazi officer let it be known around town that he wished for a dog to give him companionship. When the news came to Michael, he colored his hair black with soot, put on a new coat, and pulled his cap low over his face. Then he took up his cat and went to see the officer.

The officer handled papers on his desk. He hardly looked up. "What do you want?" he demanded.

"I have a dog to sell to you."

The officer looked up. "Do you think I am blind? That is a cat."

"It may look like a cat, sir, but I assure you that it is a rare dog indeed, a dog that will hunt like none other. No one else in the city has a dog such as this. No one in Berlin itself has such a dog."

The officer rubbed his hands with delight. "How much is the dog?"

"A dog such as this, sir, comes at no cheap price." Michael named a figure that startled the officer—it was even more than he had paid for his songbird. But he was so eager to have such a unique and rare dog—even if it did look like a skinny cat—that he paid the sum. "You must be sure to feed the dog very well at nightfall," said Michael. And the officer took the "dog" and, just before he went to sleep, fed it very well.

That night, the cat, well fed, decided that it should thank the officer for such a fine dinner. So it prowled through the house from top to bottom, hunting, and it left what it hunted in places that would be sure to please its new master. When the officer woke up, he found a dead mouse on his pillow. With a cry, he sat up and threw his blankets off—to find another dead mouse on his sheets. He put his feet into his slippers, and each slipper had a dead mouse tucked neatly into its toe. Finally he ran to his window and opened it wide. Then he grabbed the cat and flung it out the window.

The cat dropped to the ground, looked around, and then meandered down the road and back to the farm, where Michael was waiting to greet it happily.

．　．　．

Some time later, the officer let it be known around town that he wished for a horse to ride. When the news came to Michael, he stained his hair red with berries, put on a worn coat, and pulled his cap low over his face. Then he took up the harness of his donkey and went to see the officer.

The officer handled papers on his desk. He hardly looked up. "What do you want?" he demanded.

"I have a horse to sell to you."

The officer looked up, and Michael pointed out the window at his tethered donkey. "Do you think I am blind? That is a donkey."

"It may look like a donkey, sir, but I assure you that it is a rare horse indeed, a horse with legs as strong as iron. No one else in the city has a horse such as this. No one in Berlin itself has such a horse."

"Have I seen you before?" asked the officer.

"God knows if it is so," said Michael. "But you have certainly never seen a horse such as this."

The officer rubbed his hands with delight. "How much is the horse?"

"A horse such as this, sir, comes at no cheap price." Michael named a figure that startled the officer—it was even more than he had paid for his dog. But he was so eager to have such a unique and rare horse—even if it did look like a donkey—that he paid the sum. "You must be sure to stable it with its feed trough behind," said Michael. And the officer stabled the "horse" right next to his calf and placed the feed trough behind.

That night, the donkey, smelling the oats in the feed trough behind it, grew angrier and angrier that it could not reach them. When the officer came by in the morning to saddle it, the donkey lashed out first with its iron right hind foot, then with its iron left, and kicked the officer so hard that he came off the ground and struck his head on the ceiling. Howling, the officer pulled off the harness of the donkey, and pulled off the harness of the calf, and shouted them out of the stable, swearing that he would never again have anything more to do with animals.

Which was fine with the donkey and the calf. Together they trotted down the road and back to the farm, where Michael, his pockets jingling with coins, was waiting to greet them happily.

. . .

When Mara finishes the story of Michael and the Nazi officer, the children can hardly stop from laughing out loud. The mothers can hardly hold themselves back from cheering. They stuff their thin hands into their mouths, hardly daring to breathe for the laughter that wells just behind their lips.

How long has it been since laughter has come like this?

But the young girl on Mara's lap is not laughing, and she tugs at Mara's sleeve. "Michael was the name of the farmer," she says. "But what was the name of the officer?"

"People who do such things have lost their names," says Mara.

The young girl thinks about this for a while, and then asks, "But what was the name of the calf?"

Suddenly, everyone grows quiet. Mara cups her hand gently under the child's chin. "You must know the name of the calf," she whispers. "It is Israel."

The Unexpected Treasure

Eisik, the youngest boy in his family, believed that his must be one of the poorest families in all of Poland. Poorer than poor. When their Rabbi spoke of poverty, Eisik knew, he was speaking of Eisik's family. Even his hunger was hungry, and his jacket was more patch than jacket. He had seen plucked plump chickens hanging in the butcher's shop, but his mother had never, as far as Eisik knew, even been inside such a shop. He had never tasted a candy, and he wondered what one might taste like. He wondered if a house could ever be too warm. He knew that it could be too cold.

Eisik's family was very poor.

One night, Eisik dreamed that a man came to him and pointed to a bridge in Kraków. "Look by the arch of the bridge," he said, "and you will find a great treasure." Eisik woke up that morning smiling, but he knew better than to believe in a silly dream, and he soon forgot about it.

The next night the dream came again. The same man pointed to the bridge. "Look by the arch of the bridge, and you will find a great treasure." Again, Eisik woke in the morning smiling, but he knew that it was just a silly dream. He soon forgot about it.

On the third night, the man came again into his dreams, and now he was angry. "Do I come all the way into the World of Confusion for nothing every night?" he demanded. "Now, boy, look by the arch of the bridge, and you will find a great treasure."

When Eisik woke, he was trembling. He went to his mother and asked if she believed that dreams can come true. She leaned down and kissed him on the forehead. "Of course they can come true. Weren't you born to us?"

Eisik packed some food and set off for Kraków.

It was a long walk, and the sun was well on its way to rest before Eisik reached the city and found the bridge. He scrambled down the embankment and onto a slate walk. It was slimy with the damp of the water, so he crept slowly, looking into all the shadows, testing the bricks to see if they might give and the treasure be hidden behind them. But there was nothing at all. Tired and wet, he climbed back up to the bridge.

"You there! What are you doing?" A swastikaed guard. Eisik froze.

"What are you doing, creeping about the bridge like that?"

And Eisik, scared and ashamed, could only say, "It was a dream. A dream told me I should do it."

"A dream? A dream?" The guard laughed. "Don't you know better than to believe in a silly dream? Don't you know that dreams mean nothing? Why, these last three nights, I've had the same dream again and again: A man comes and tells me that there is a great treasure hidden under the stove in the house of a poor family with a boy named Eisik. Do you see me running off, looking into

48

every Jewish house with a boy named Eisik and digging under their stove? Do you?"

Eisik shook his head, but his heart stopped.

The guard flourished his rifle at him. "Off now, and don't trouble me with dreams."

Eisik sprinted from the bridge and ran out of Kraków all the way home, where his father and mother and brothers and sisters were waiting for him. They threw their arms around him, and his mother wept, and even his father. "We thought . . ." they began, and could not go on. They feared to say aloud what they had thought in the World of Confusion where anything at all might happen.

And when they had all gone inside, Eisik and his father moved their iron stove. They pried up a layer of bricks, and beneath it they found a box filled with gold and silver coins. It was enough, said Papa, to get all of them, even Grandpapa and Tante, out of Poland. Maybe even to America.

And Eisik hoped that that dream would come true as well.

Living and Dancing

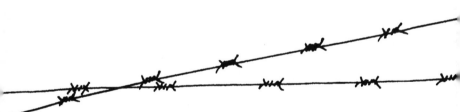

When Mara looks out at those listening to her stories, she wonders what they see. There was a time about a thousand, thousand years ago when she had full red hair that could not be hidden under any kerchief. In the sun, it glowed like a sunrise, and her father told her that God had been too generous on the day she was born. Her fingers were long and supple, and though everyone told her she should learn to play the piano she preferred the breathy sounds of the flute, the running of her fingers down its silvery length. And her eyes held a startling pool of darkness, the color of the richest chocolate, and though her mother would cup her face in one hand, smile, and say those eyes were too close together, she knew they were just right.

Mara can remember nights when she would dance with the other girls and her hair would flame out, her hands wave to the rhythm, her eyes fairly sing with the pleasure of the circle. Her feet would follow the complexity of the steps all on their own, and her knees would bend as if she had no say in it—they must bend because the movement of the *music told them so. Some nights when she danced, she could hardly breathe.*

Now it is all mostly a memory. But once after they returned to the barracks, Mara got off her bunk and began to dance the dances she remembered so well. Her hair was no longer red, her fingers were cracked and stubbly, and her eyes dulled. But her dancing! Her dancing!

And afterward, when she had danced to a music no one else had heard, she told a story.

The Dance

In the Polish city of Dombrowa, Rabbi Haim gathered together his disciples into his house in the last days before they would flee. Already many of his disciples had been arrested and sent away—only God knew where. Some had simply been murdered in their homes by those who looked forward to the coming Nazi triumph.

And so the group that gathered around Rabbi Haim was very still and very quiet.

When they had prayed, the Rabbi saw that they were all half looking over their shoulders and starting at every noise that they heard from the streets. Their eyes were red with no sleep. Their hands shook, and their lips trembled. So the Rabbi passed the wine around and said, "Now, we dance." The disciples looked around at one another fearfully. "And who will play for us?" asked the Rabbi.

But none of the disciples moved. What if someone from the outside should hear them? Rabbi Haim looked at them sorrowfully, but with understanding.

"In the world of evil," he said quietly, "only trust and faith matter. Only trust and faith. And when these are gone, all joy is gone. And when joy is gone, then has the evil truly won."

A long moment passed then, and as the Divine Presence held her sweet breath, one by one, the disciples stood. One went for the violin, another for the oboe. They grasped one another's hands, and they began to dance. At first they all circled slowly, slowly, and then faster and faster, until the dancing filled the room and the music spiced the heated air.

Down below, the Rabbi's wife looked up the stairs fearfully. They must be drunk, she thought. Why else would they dance now, and play so loudly that anyone might hear them in the street? She paced back and forth, back and forth, checking time and again to be sure that the front door was bolted, hoping that no one would hear what anyone with ears could hear.

When the Rabbi came out with an empty jug for more wine, she held her hands to him as if in prayer. "You must stop dancing," she begged. "Anyone in the street can hear you."

"You are right," he said. "You go and tell them."

The Rabbi's wife raced up the stairs and opened the door. But what she saw silenced her. The disciples danced in a wide circle, and leaping in and out and among them was a blazing ribbon of blue fire whose sparkle lit the room and tingled all the air.

The Rabbi's wife went back downstairs. She took the jug from her husband and filled it with red wine. She sent him back upstairs.

Then she unbolted the front door.

From the Stones

One morning in the Jewish ghetto, when the sun rose cold and pale, four Nazi trucks drove onto the main street, smoking in the wintry air. Before they had even stopped, their storm troopers leapt out of the backs and, machine guns at the ready, rushed into the quiet houses. Screams filled the streets as the drivers stood together, sharing cigarettes and laughing. Then the doors opened, and men and boys stumbled out. They held their hands above their heads. Only a few had coats on. Some were half dressed, some barefoot.

The storm troopers said nothing but with their machine guns forced the men and boys onto the trucks. The prisoners looked back at the wives and mothers they had left. The wives and mothers wept.

The four trucks drove from the ghetto, faster, it seemed, than the narrow old streets could ever have allowed. No one spoke while the storm troopers watched, but those in the backs of the trucks saw that they were coming to a part of the town they had once known well, the Jewish quarter of the city. They strained to see the old landmarks, the homes that they had cherished, the shops and markets they had visited, the House of Prayer.

But when they saw them, they looked away. Better to let a memory live in the air than see it as a shattered and ruined reality.

Abruptly, the trucks stopped and the storm troopers jumped out again. *"Schnell! Schnell!"* they cried, Hurry! Hurry!, and the men and boys, their hands once again over their heads, came out by the old Jewish cemetery. Against the stone wall was a line of picks and sledgehammers, and in front of them stood a German officer, warm in a heavy coat, his hands clasped behind his back.

"A line! Form a line!" called the storm troopers, and when their prisoners had formed the line, the German officer spoke.

"Work detail, the German army has need of new roads to support its legions of tanks. And for new roads, there must be new paving material, new stone." He smiled and pointed behind him into the cemetery. "You will find the stone in there."

"Schnell! Schnell!" cried the storm troopers again, and with gun butts pushed the men and boys to the picks and sledgehammers. Their handles felt like bones as they bore them into the cemetery.

But here was the place they had stood so often to recite the last prayers. Every one of them could find his own family name on many of the stones. It was as if they were to take hammers to themselves.

No one moved. No one lifted the picks.

A shot, and one of the boys jerked forward to his knees, and then onto his face. His blood smeared blackly against one of the stones.

"*Schnell!*"

And so, horrified, weeping, they began, as the storm troopers behind them smoked their cigarettes. A swing of a sledgehammer, and a tombstone broke into three pieces, thudding to the ground like a broken heart. A swing of a pick, and another tombstone cracked, wobbled, then fell to dust. A swing, and a candelabrum's delicate branches were smashed. A swing, and spiraling columns were obliterated. The stones broke open and sent their ancient dust up into the air, where the winter wind caught it and blew it away. Anyone's heart would break, seeing it.

But that was not all that went up into the air.

"Look," whispered a boy. "Just look."

And when they looked, they saw that the names on the stones were not shattering to ruin but were flying into the air above them. They watched as the names rushed from the stones, as they jostled themselves into a wide circle and then came together in a great dance whose rhythms defied the buffets of the winter wind. They danced and danced, the circle growing larger and larger as more and more names flew up, the dancing growing wilder and wilder until, as the last stone cracked, the names spiraled higher and higher and were lost in the sudden holy blue of heaven.

Questions Angels
Fear to Ask

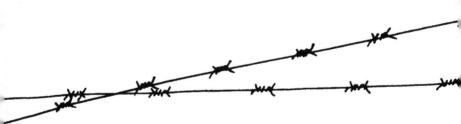

*O*f all Mara's stories, the stories of escape are the most exciting. Everyone in the barracks knows of someone who has tried to escape, and these tales strike at them like hammers. But Mara tells them over and over again, and every time there is still the same tingle of fear—but also the same lovely hope.

Often in Mara's stories the escapes fail, and these stories scour the women with terrible loss. But if in these stories occasionally someone, perhaps a rabbi, can escape from the darkness, who knows but that someone else might as well? Who knows if someone the women love is even now preparing the sabbath meal in a safe place, and saying a prayer for those left behind? Who knows?

The Three Men

All over Europe, Jews fled the Nazi shadow as it blotted out light after light after light. And all over Europe, at the same time that men and women and children were rounded up and sent to unspeakable places, there were miracles of preservation and rescue. Who can tell how both these things can be true?

The Belzer Rabbi—long life to him—had waited as the shadow darkened around him and around those under his care. "Leave, Rabbi," they said to him. "Leave now." But he waited until almost everyone else had left. On his last day in Belz, he sat alone in his House of Prayer, cradling the Torah in his arms. Then, finally, he walked out of the House and closed the doors behind him. He knew he would never see its eastern wall again.

Waiting outside was a car, a plume of smoke hovering around it like a cloud. One of his students, Felix, got out and held the door open for him. The Rabbi touched the closed doors of his House of Prayer and, without looking back, walked to the car and clambered in, awkward with the Torah. He could not see for his tears.

"Rabbi," said Felix, "already the Nazis are searching for you. Here, look. They have pasted posters around the town square with your picture."

The Rabbi looked at the dark picture of himself. "I should look so bad?"

"Rabbi, it is close enough to recognize. Here is a bowl and water and a razor. I am afraid . . . Rabbi, I am sorry but I am afraid that I must ask you . . ."

The Rabbi held up his hand. "So I must look like the goyim. Eh, worse could happen. Not much worse, but worse." Felix waited impatiently while the Rabbi shaved in the backseat of the car; then he drove out of town and to the west.

It was not long before they came to the first checkpoint straddling the road. "Rabbi," warned Felix.

"We are in God's hands," answered the Rabbi, and it must have been so, because as they slowed, the guards seemed not to see them. Felix never even stopped but slowly rolled through, hardly daring to breathe.

"Rabbi," said Felix, "how can it be that they did not stop us?"

"Drive ahead," the Rabbi answered.

They passed through four more checkpoints, and at each one, the same thing happened. Cars would be stopped in front of and behind them, but as Felix came to the checkpoint, he would drive slowly through, not breathing each time, and the guards seemed not even to see them.

Toward nightfall, Felix had to stop for rest, and he pulled the car to the side of the road and got out. He stretched his legs, his arms, and kneaded the soreness out of his back. He lifted his face to the gathering coolness of the dusk. A single star shone low over the horizon, and it gladdened him.

He turned back to the car.

He could not see it.

It could be no more than a few paces away, but he could not see it.

The Rabbi would not have driven away. And if he had, then Felix would have heard. Felix reached into his pocket; there were the keys.

"Rabbi!" Felix shouted. "Rabbi, are you there? Rabbi!"

He heard a car door open and saw the Rabbi step out. "Shush, shush! Are you calling all the German army, or just half?"

Felix took a few steps forward and reached out. His hand passed through a warm cloud and touched the open car door. "Rabbi," he said wonderingly, "there is a cloud around the car that hides it."

"This you should know only now?" answered the Rabbi.

But the cloud did not hide words, and a German soldier, drawn by the sound of Felix's shouts, stepped out from the woods he had been searching. In one hand, he held a rifle that he fixed on the Rabbi; in the other, he held the leash of a straining, eager dog.

"The Belzer Rabbi," the soldier said simply, and grinned. The Rabbi held Felix by the arm and said nothing.

The soldier came closer to them, the dog pulling him forward, its ears flat back. It snarled, and the soldier said again, "The Belzer Rabbi."

And at that moment, three men stepped from behind the cloud that hid the car. They looked tired, as if they had traveled a long way. They walked between the Rabbi and the soldier, and though they did not wear uniforms, the soldier saluted them. The dog cowered.

"Let him pass," said the tallest of the three men. The soldier nodded and stepped back.

The smallest one, the youngest one, turned to Felix and smiled. "Go," he said sweetly. Felix wanted to laugh aloud at the lovely music of his voice, the play of light in his eyes.

But Felix only nodded, and taking the arm of the Rabbi, he led him into the still-invisible car. He felt his way to the front, started the engine, and drove away.

The Rabbi no longer was weeping. True enough, he no longer could sit by his eastern wall. But there would come another, and while he waited, he would be in God's hands.

Which Shoebox?

Abraham's mother held him tightly by the shoulders. She stared deeply into his face.

"A Jew must always be ready to leave quickly," she said.

Abraham nodded.

"A Jew must be ready to pick up a satchel and walk out the door."

"Yes," Abraham said.

"It has always been so for us."

"And is it so now?" asked Abraham.

"Yes, it is so now. Now more than ever. Go upstairs and pack one of the shoeboxes under your bed. Put it in a place where you can grab it in just a moment."

Abraham went upstairs and looked under his bed. He pulled out not one but two shoeboxes and set them on his desk. Into the first he put three pairs of socks, two pairs of underwear, three handkerchiefs, a tightly rolled scarf, and a pair of woolen mittens. Then he closed the box and tied it with a string.

Into the second box he put a picture of himself with his mama and his papa. He put a letter his grandpapa had written to him after his Bar Mitzvah. He put his favorite book of fairy tales inside, a handful of marbles in a leather bag, and a coin his grandmama had given him and which he would never, never spend because she had given it to him. Then he closed the box and tied it with a string.

That night, Abraham awoke to the splintering sounds of smashed glass. Shots ricocheted in the distance, and then more broken glass quite close by. Another smashing, then heavy, thick laughter, and someone was in his father's shop downstairs, calling out something terrible and crashing everything to the floor.

His mother rushed into his room. She was already dressed and held Abraham's coat. His father stood behind her with a satchel.

"Is it time to leave quickly?" Abraham asked.

"Yes," said his mother. "We must leave very quickly."

Abraham put on his coat and grabbed his shoebox. Then they went down the back stairs, sprinted across the empty lot behind the house, and walked quickly in the darkness, away from the splintering glass, away from their life.

Only in the morning did Abraham realize that he had brought the wrong box.

Shards

Is there a greater sin than the sin of betrayal?

Once in the city of Rizhyn, there was a man named Shmulik who was never happy. He was never happy, he thought, because he never had enough money. If only I had the money to do this, he would think, then I too would be considered one of the great ones in the House of Prayer. If only I had enough money to do that, he would think, then everyone in Rizhyn would listen to what I have to tell them. Instead, I am a nothing. No one ever listens.

He brooded on his sorrow day after day and night after night, until his sorrow grew greater than anything else in his life.

At that time, Jewish families began to be deported from Rizhyn, and many went into hiding. Some families had prepared well-stocked bunkers beneath their homes or in abandoned buildings nearby. Others paid Christian families to be hidden in tiny attic rooms. Others, who had believed that the deportations could never come to Rizhyn, remained in their homes and were quickly found.

But even those who had gone into hiding were not safe. Not a day went by without some bunker being discovered—no matter how cleverly hidden, no matter how ingeniously concealed. And what happened to those found hidden there, even to the children, was never talked about.

Soon, there were almost no Jews left in the city of Rizhyn. Only the Rabbi and those closest to him remained, and though the Nazis searched day after day they could not find him, because his bunker had been prepared for him in secret. Only two or three souls had ever known where it was, and they had left Rizhyn before the deportations. But still the search went on, from one house to another. And though the Rabbi, his family, and the few disciples left to him trembled when they heard the sounds of steps above them, they knew that they would never be found.

Until one day, the Rabbi heard the familiar voice of Shmulik calling softly. "Rabbi! Rabbi! Are you here? Rabbi!"

And the Rabbi called back to him. "Shmulik, Shmulik, is that you?"

"Yes, Rabbi. It is I, Shmulik. Where are you?"

The Rabbi touched a lever and pushed open a paneled door. "Here, Shmulik. Come inside quickly."

Shmulik went inside. The Rabbi was surprised at how fine Shmulik looked. He wore clothes better than any he had ever worn before, and he was fatter. There even seemed to be a film of grease around his mouth.

"Shmulik, what have you done?"

"People listen to me now, Rabbi."

"Shmulik, empty your pockets and hold out to me what you have."

Shmulik hesitated. Then he reached inside his pocket and pulled out a handful of gold coins that glowed even in the darkness of the bunker.

"So, Shmulik," said the Rabbi quietly, "how long shall we wait until you bring the Nazi murderers back?"

Shmulik said nothing. With a firm arm, the Rabbi turned him around and shoved him out of the bunker. The paneling closed behind him.

When it closed, Shmulik began to weep. He could not stop. He began to weep and weep with the terrible, unforgivable burden of what he had done. And when he walked outside to the waiting patrol, he looked down at his hands and found that the gold coins had become clay shards.

God in Court

In the darkness and loneliness of his ruined apartment, Feivel stood with his hands clenched and raised in accusation. The tears that heated his cheeks came without stopping, and his trembling lips writhed in sorrow.

That night, when the roundup had begun, he had hidden his wife and daughter behind the false wall of the closet. And then, since there was no more space for him, he had fled. Now, just before dawn, he had come back to the apartment that had been looted. Nothing that was his remained.

And his wife, his beautiful wife was gone.

And his daughter, his delight, his laughing daughter was gone.

Toward morning, Feivel went in search of the Rabbi and his court. The search took him most of the morning. The streets were filled with broken glass, spilled suitcases, papers, discarded clothing, and shell cases. Many shell cases. Feivel darted from doorway to doorway, searching for the Rabbi, and after several hours, he found him in a dank basement, surrounded by those who remained of his court. They were all silent, and some did not even look up when Feivel came in. Not until he spoke.

"Rabbi," said Feivel, "I have a suit to bring against God."

Then they all looked up with horror in their eyes.

"A suit to bring against God?" whispered the Rabbi.

"Yes, Rabbi, a suit against God."

Again silence, except for something dripping. The Rabbi seemed to count the drips as he considered.

"And what is this suit that you would bring against God?" asked the Rabbi. It seemed that the Rabbi was almost fearful of what Feivel would say.

And Feivel was fearful himself. To accuse God! But then he thought about the streets and the shell cases. And about his apartment, his beautiful wife, and the laughter of his daughter. And his heart began to thud and thud so loudly, and with such strength, that he felt it must burst through his chest.

"Rabbi," said Feivel, "it is written in the Torah that the children of Israel will always and forever be God's servants. Is this how one treats a servant? Even the very worst of servants? And now that He has scattered us all across the lands, He does not even allow us to be His servants. He does not allow those whom we love to live. He does not even allow us to live. That is my suit."

And Feivel began to weep, and all the court was silent, for Feivel's tears were themselves the strongest accusation.

Then the Rabbi held up his hand. "Enough. The plaintiff and the defendant must now leave the room so that the Court may consider the suit. So go now, Feivel. And Lord of all the Universe, we cannot send out one whose presence is everywhere and every time. But we tell You now that we will not let Your presence influence us for even the smallest of moments."

Feivel, his face in his hands, went outside, back onto the street. A wind blew down and swirled around him for a moment, surprisingly warm, then passed on. Feivel waited and waited, standing in such full view that any patrol which might have driven by would have seen and arrested him. Or perhaps it would have just shot him, a moment of laughter for them. Feivel would not have minded.

Then the door opened and he was summoned back inside. Now every eye watched him, and Feivel saw that the Rabbi's eyes were wet.

"Feivel," said the Rabbi, "do you persist in this suit?"

Feivel nodded. "I do, Rabbi."

The Rabbi sighed, and it seemed as if a groan came out of the court.

The Rabbi closed his eyes. "Then the Court finds . . ." He paused, and took a deep breath. "The Court finds that Feivel is in the right."

The Tsaddik, *One Righteous Soul*

There are times when the fate of the whole world hinges upon one righteous soul.

.　.　.

Wherever Hitler ordered them to go, his armies pushed triumphantly from one country into another, like a horrid, bloated spider thrusting to the east and west and north and even south. In its drive across the desert, the Afrika Korps of General Rommel took anything that Hitler wanted. And he wanted everything.

So in the land of Palestine, in Jerusalem itself, fear spread that Nazi troops might someday enter the Holy City.

On a day when the Afrika Korps was pushing toward the border of Palestine, and when all of Jerusalem was beginning to panic and many had already fled, a Rabbi went to the old cemetery to pray by the grave of the Or ha-Haim, a *tsaddik*, a righteous man, who had died long ago. The Rabbi's disciples came with him, but as they stood around the grave murmuring the prayers, they could not help but look fearfully behind them, listening for the hollow sound of tank fire that would announce the coming of the Afrika Korps. They were amazed that the Rabbi seemed so very calm, so unaware of anything but the prayers for the Or ha-Haim.

Together they sang a psalm, and then they were finished. The Rabbi bent down slowly to kiss the gravestone, and when he stood, his own eyes so full of peace, he looked at his disciples, saw them wringing their hands, saw them looking over their shoulders, saw them starting at any noise, and asked, "What is it?"

"Please, Rabbi, please pray."

"I have just prayed."

"Pray that Rommel does not come to Jerusalem. Pray that he does not cross into Palestine. Please, Rabbi, please pray for us all."

For a very long time, the Rabbi stood by the grave of the Or ha-Haim. It was very quiet. Now his students looked at nothing but him. They listened for nothing but his next words.

Finally he spoke. "Rommel will not come to Palestine," he said. "He will not enter the Holy City." And the disciples believed.

On that very day, many miles away from Jerusalem, the Americans fought the Afrika Korps in a great and terrible battle. They stopped Rommel's advance.

He will never enter the Holy City.

. . .

There are times when the fate of the whole world—the whole world—hinges upon one righteous soul.

A Bleak Hope

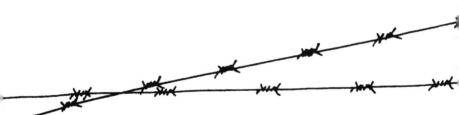

Not everyone always understands Mara's stories, and sometimes the listeners go to sleep at night disquieted, as though something worse than the beating and the hunger has come upon them, something worse than dying.

But if Mara tells such a fearsome tale one night, she is sure to tell a very different one the next, as if she has somehow purged herself and is now ready again to tell a story of light and warmth—even when she tells stories about the death camps themselves.

The "Good Morning"

Every warm morning for years and years and years, Herr Shaul left his home, stood for a moment to smell the sun in the air, and strolled down his street. It was a small street, lined by small houses. But each house was bright and tidy, and some, like Herr Mueller's, had carefully planted flower gardens out front.

Herr Shaul would walk slowly, examining each garden, watching to see if any of the new red tulips had opened, if the roses had budded yet, if all the daffodils had passed or if one or two yellow blossoms still stuck out their slender orange tongues.

And every morning, when Herr Shaul passed, Herr Mueller would be on his knees in the garden, planting a seedling he had nursed through the late winter, spading over the dark soil, or carefully separating a grouping of lily bulbs, laying aside those he thought would no longer bloom and replanting the others.

Herr Mueller was very careful about his selection.

"Good morning, Herr Mueller," Herr Shaul would say.

Herr Mueller would look up from his work and smile. "Good morning, Herr Shaul," he would answer, and touch his cap to him.

That was all. "Good morning, Herr Mueller." "Good morning, Herr Shaul." They had greeted each other a thousand times, several thousand times. It was a ritual that only they shared.

But on this spring day, Herr Shaul was not walking down his street and stopping at the garden. Twelve days ago he had left all that behind him, and he knew that he would never see it again. After being hauled out of his house at night and loaded into a crammed truck, he had spent a chaotic two days under guard at the train station—

under guard like a criminal—four days in a stifling cattle car with only a corner to sleep against, another three days in a train station, then another three—or was it four?—in another cattle car.

He had survived by remembering his strolls past the flower gardens.

Now he was taking another stroll, but this one at a shuffle. As it was, he could not have walked any faster. Guards screamed at him to hurry, but he could not. He was so thirsty and so terribly hungry. I have not combed my hair in all this time, he thought. And I have been wearing the same clothes.

More shuffling, and he passed through the barbed-wire fences of the death camp. He shuddered as the shadows of the fence posts fell against him. He tried to wet his lips, but even his tongue was dry.

Ahead of him, the line separated into two. To the left shuffled the old ones like himself, so weak, drooping like wilted daffodils. To the right younger ones, ones who might be made to work for the murderers.

Herr Shaul saw and understood. He thought for a moment of trying to square his shoulders, of trying to summon up everything in him so that he might pass to the right. But he could not, and his mind went back to his morning walks as he shuffled farther into the camp.

The two lines angled from a desk that stood in the center of the compound like a small fortress. A phalanx of guards poised behind it, their faces showing nothing, their stone hands holding machine guns. They had seen the ritual of this division a thousand times. One yawned widely as Herr Shaul shuffled toward them.

Are the demons in hell bored? Herr Shaul wondered.

Then he looked down at the Nazi officer sitting behind the desk, the man selecting who was to go to which side. His uniform was perfect, not a crease out of place, not a button that was dull. The zigzag lines of his insignia gleamed. And before he had even thought, before he had even recognized, Herr Shaul said, "Good morning, Herr Mueller."

And the Nazi officer looked up, and before he had even thought, before he had even recognized, he said, "Good morning, Herr Shaul."

A pause, and Herr Shaul felt the pressure of the shuffling line build up behind him. A small flicker in Herr Mueller's eyes—could it be shame? Just for a moment, could it be shame?

Herr Mueller jerked his thumb. "To the right," he said.

The Wonder

Chaim had been in the camp for less than three days before he woke one morning to realize that he could no longer believe in God. And who could blame him? Could you or I? Could God Himself blame him?

Chaim felt empty, and fought to stay that way. He was afraid of what might fill him. The putrid smell of the gas that hovered over the camp like the fog of a swamp. The buzzing, the unbearable buzzing of the flies that moved in clouds among the pits behind the barracks. The shots, all through the day, all through the night. The beatings. He could close his eyes, but he would still hear the thud of a truncheon on bone, or the snap of a whip across a face.

Or what was even worse, he might be filled with

the last sight of his father and his mouthed words to him: "Go with God."

Chaim roused himself in the darkness. The world was dark, and darkness was all there was. But still, it was his job this morning to carry the soup for the barracks, and it was time. He hoped that he could haul it back without spilling. If he spilled, there would be nothing for him but a beating from a *kapo*. He walked outside in the freezing cold and stood there with other boys and with old men, and when his turn came to take the vat, he put out his hands and saw that the man who would help him carry the soup back to the barracks was his own Rabbi.

"Chaim," the Rabbi said, but Chaim could not look at his Rabbi's face.

Together they hefted the vat and lugged it out the door and into the cold. The thin steam of it curled up around them, and they struggled and slipped in the mud.

"Chaim," whispered the Rabbi gently, "He is the All and Ever Present. He is here, even here in this place."

The Rabbi knew. Somehow or other, he knew.

"My father," said Chaim.

"Yes," the Rabbi said, nodding. "We have all of us lost fathers."

"Rabbi, I can no longer believe. God is hiding."

A long moment. The Rabbi shifted the weight of the vat from one hand to the other. "The moment we know Him to be hiding, then He ceases to be hiding," he replied.

"I have seen the world, Rabbi. I have seen the world, and I know that God cannot be here. And if He is not here with us in this place, then He is not anywhere."

They were almost to the barracks now, where the ground was its muddiest. The vat was becoming impossibly heavy for Chaim, and even the Rabbi grunted with the effort of carrying it.

"So what would God have to do, young Chaim, for one such as you who has seen the world to believe again?"

"A wonder, Rabbi. God would have to make a wonder."

At the door of the barracks the *kapo* waited, slapping the black truncheon into the palm of his hand. Chaim steadied the vat and placed his feet carefully in the mud. But when they were just two or three steps from the *kapo,* the Rabbi stumbled, and the soup sloshed out of the vat and onto the shins of the *kapo* himself.

Chaim waited for the first blows. He knew that the Rabbi would die, and perhaps he would too. He was almost eager for it to be finished.

But the moment passed. Then another, and another. The *kapo* stared past them, still slapping the truncheon into the palm of his hand. The Rabbi steadied himself, Chaim changed hands, and then together they brought the soup into the barracks.

Chaim looked up at the Rabbi with wonder in his eyes. The Rabbi put his hand behind Chaim's head and drew his forehead against his own. "You see, young Chaim," he whispered, "even here in this place."

The Rod

Adolf Hitler stood on the coast of France, the waves frothing beneath him, the wind that had come all the way across the sea from America whipping their tops. His hands were clenched. He had beaten every European army, had made even England's might flee back across the Channel. Now he looked at the cliffs of England itself, only a handful, a short handful of kilometers away.

And he could not get there.

He turned to his generals, who trembled when they saw Hitler's eyes upon them. "How will you get my armies across?" he demanded.

None of them answered.

"How will you get my armies across?" he roared.

"There is a foolish Jewish legend," one general stammered, "that Moses opened a path in the sea."

Adolf Hitler looked back across the Channel. "How did he do it?"

"He struck the sea with a rod."

"And where is this rod?"

"It is only a legend, Führer. But there is a Rabbi we are holding in Paris who might know."

"Bring the Rabbi here," Adolf Hitler said. His eyes did not leave the Channel. His hands were still clenched.

The call went out, and that night the Rabbi was awakened, hustled to a waiting car, and driven at breakneck speed to the coast of France, where Adolf Hitler was waiting. Pulled out of the car, the Rabbi was shoved to the bluff.

The beauty of the Channel almost over-whelmed the Rabbi. He held his arms up and his hands open to receive it. The blue and green and white and gray of the sea. The gulls riding the bil-lowing air and calling out in their ecstasy. The fresh brine on the breezes. How marvelous are all Thy works, O God our God! thought the Rabbi.

But Adolf Hitler had stood on the coast all night, and now he reached out and shook the Rabbi.

"There is a legend that your Moses struck the sea and opened a path through it."

"There is such a story of Moses."

"And he struck the sea with a rod."

The Rabbi nodded. "It is written that he struck the sea with a rod."

"Then, Jew, tell me where that rod is. Tell me, and I shall set you free."

"And this is something that is in your hands to do?" asked the Rabbi.

"Where is the rod?"

"Herr Hitler, you are going to have a hard time getting it."

"Tell me!"

The Rabbi pointed across the Channel. "In London, Herr Hitler. The rod is in the British Museum."

Miracles Covered
with Ashes

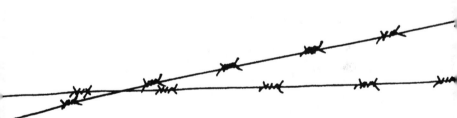

As Mara tells the stories during the dark nights, as they brighten the cold air, her face transforms. It happens every time.

It may be that she has spent that day hefting stones from one pile to another. It may be that she has dug in a muddy trench for all the daylight hours. It may be that she has carried bodies to stack like a cord of wood.

She may come into the barracks with a face of torn stone, so hard that she cannot talk, her eyes shut so that she cannot see. Sometimes when the women and children start to come around her for a story, she holds her hands out. "I have nothing to give tonight," she says. "I have no more stories to give." But they still come and sit silently near her, waiting. And finally the stone face crumbles, and Mara wipes at her eyes, takes a child onto her lap, and begins.

On nights like that, when it seems as if Mara has no more to give, she tells the most beautiful stories, the stories most full of light and warmth.

And when she finishes, she has become alive again.

Keep Tight Hold

All nights in the Janowski Road Camp were dark and cold. And all nights brought the demons and the guards—who is to say which were which?

But this night was the darkest, and the coldest, and the most demonic that Adam had ever seen.

In one moment, guards and dogs had burst into the barracks, shouting, screaming, beating, until all was a screeching confusion. Five hundred souls had fled outside, calling for sons, for brothers, for friends, all flooded away in a wave of terrible fear. And Adam, who felt his hand gripped by his father, went flooding out on the very crest, his father's shoulder taking the blow meant for him at the barracks door.

Through the darkness they ran in bare feet, booted guards pacing easily alongside, dogs snapping at the slow. They ran weeping into the dark, the stars hidden from them by clouds blacker than night, until the trees suddenly came upon them like stone pillars.

Past the trees—

"*Schnell! Schnell!*"

—and then into a clearing, where they stopped, their breath wrenching from them and hovering in a ghastly cloud.

In front of them yawned an open pit, huge, so black that the bottom was invisible, the other side only dimly seen, it was so far away.

Silence. Silence in the dark. Silence in the cold.

Adam felt his father grip his hand very tightly.

The guards, holding machine guns up to their shoulders, lined their prisoners along the side of the pit. The guards were smiling. Adam shivered at the sight out of hell. He felt a groan rising from those around him, a groan of hopelessness. When he looked up, he was surprised to see a few stars.

He felt the grip of his father and asked, "What is going to happen to us?"

And then the shots began. A burst of shots, the thud of bodies falling, a pause, and then another burst of shots.

Adam looked into his father's face and saw a tear. "Today, Adam," he said, "today we will be in the World of Truth." He nodded, even smiled, and Adam drew close to his father and listened to the shots.

"I'm cold," he said.

"Do you remember when Mama went into town and bought us the red woolen coats? The red ones with the black stripes? And do you remember how warm and scratchy they were? We'll pretend that we are wearing Mama's coats now, and that we are as warm as when we wore them last winter."

Adam, standing by his father, felt warmer. But the shots kept coming, and coming and coming, until now they were very close, and the sound of the thudding bodies was terrible to hear, even more terrible than the shots.

"Adam, do you see the far side?"

Adam nodded. More stars had pierced the murk of the clouds and shone brightly.

"The Baal Shem Tov was once pursued by those who hated him. And when he came to a river he could not cross, he threw his belt across the water and walked across on his great faith in the God of Israel alone. When the Adversary comes to us, Adam, at our beginnings, our turnings, and our endings, it is him over whom we must jump."

"We have no belt," said Adam, simply.

"So we will rely on our faith alone. Keep tight hold of my hand. Close your eyes, Adam. And when I tell you to jump, jump far."

Adam closed his eyes. He felt his father kiss the top of his head.

And the shots came closer, and closer, and closer. Until they were so very close, and then they were right upon them. Adam felt the heat of the gun move behind his head, and he trembled.

Then he heard his father whisper, "Adam, jump," and he gathered himself, opened his eyes once more to see the stars—there was a great host of them now—and jumped into their light.

It seemed to Adam that he jumped a long way, and that the light of the stars was very bright. He had to close his eyes against it.

When his feet felt the earth again, he opened his eyes. Adam was still holding tight to his father's hand. He looked around. They had jumped over the pit, over the clearing, and well into the trees on the far side.

They were wearing warm and scratchy red woolen coats.

Together, still holding hands, they ran deeper into the woods. Behind them, there was a burst of shots, a pause, a burst of shots, a pause, a burst of shots, a pause . . .

The Miracle

The forest was very, very quiet. The guards had marched away, their guns still warm. The sounds of shots that had echoed off bare trunks had flown away into the air, into thin air. And the cries, the prayers had flown up to heaven.

Now there was only quiet. Not even the birds cawed. Not even the wind blew. It was as still as if the whole world had stopped spinning and died.

In the great pit that slashed across the clearing, nothing moved. The murdered bodies that filled it were quiet too. For a time, a leg had stretched out, a head had looked up with bleeding eyes, but even that was finished.

There was only the quiet.

Then, a gust of wind came out of the first purple of dawn, and with it came walking none other than the great Rabbi, the Baal Shem Tov. The Baal Shem Tov himself, who comes into all generations. Two centuries ago he had wandered Poland, and it was said that he wore miracles like a cloak. He healed the sick, brought a child to the childless couple, found the horse that had run away, rescued the unjustly accused. The Baal Shem Tov brought miracles where they were needed, where they had to happen.

Slowly the Baal Shem Tov walked across the clearing and stood at the edge of the pit. He stood very still.

Nothing moved. His searching eyes reached across.

Nothing moved. His lips began to murmur a prayer, and the angels bent down to listen.

But nothing moved.

And then an arm, shaking and pale, reached up to him from out of the desolation. Then another, and another. They reached, trembling, fingers shaking. As the Baal Shem Tov watched, arm after arm reached in the growing light. In the sunrise, the arms were red with light—or blood.

And then the miracle came. As quietly as the sunrise, the miracle came. But it did not come from the Baal Shem Tov. The miracle came from the pit. Slowly, voices rose, rose and mingled. They grew louder, and louder still, as the Baal Shem Tov stood by the pit's edge.

"Welcome," the voices said slowly, with the dry voices of the old, the cheery calls of the young. "Welcome to the Rabbi Israel Baal Shem Tov. Welcome, welcome, and thank you for your miracles. Thank you for your miracles."

And that was all. The voices ceased, the arms fell back. And the Baal Shem Tov—may his merits shield us—was left alone in the gathering brightness of the forest.

It was very quiet.

The Promise of the Talis Koten

For almost thirty days, Noah had worked in hell. He knew that he would not be there for much longer. The Nazis of Auschwitz forced Jews to do the dreadful work of the gas chambers for only thirty days, and then the workers themselves would die in them.

Noah prayed that the thirty days would pass quickly. Since he had brought out the bodies of his little sisters, since he had kissed their cheeks, since he had sent his soul from out of his own body, he had prayed with everything still left in him that the thirty days would pass quickly.

And now the doors to the chambers opened, and Noah made his face turn blank, made his eyes not see what must be seen. The smell of the gas billowed out, and with it the smells of sweat and urine—the scent of death. Noah felt himself move forward with others, felt himself reach out to the bodies that still stood upright, so tightly had they been packed into the chamber—oh God, so tightly—and felt himself pry the first body away and carry it to the waiting carts.

"God," he prayed, "make the days pass quickly."

"*Schnell!*" called the guards.

Yes, hurry, thought Noah.

When he was almost finished, Noah saw the next mass of souls pushed toward the gas chambers. They were naked. The men's beards had been shaved, and their cheeks looked starkly white. "Showers, only showers," the guards were calling out, but among the souls, someone was singing the *kaddish:* "May His great name be magnified and sanctified." Most were silent. They held their arms tightly around themselves, as if to keep their bodies and souls together.

Noah watched but did not watch. He could not let his eyes see this thing.

But sometimes we are meant to see the thing that must be seen.

Noah's eyes cleared and sharpened, and he saw an old, a very old man clutching his prayer shawl, the worn fringes of it tight in his grasp. He stared at Noah and then beckoned to him with a trembling hand. Noah's hands began to tremble as well, the touch of death still cold upon them. But he went to the old man.

"I know where I am going," he said to Noah.

Noah could say nothing.

"I know where I am going. I ask only one thing of you. One thing." He looked down to his prayer shawl and stroked it once. "When I am dead, I ask you should put this on me. Burn my body together with my *talis koten*. You can do this?"

Noah stared at the old man. "But why?" he asked hopelessly.

And the old man smiled. "My dear son, because of this: Even if nothing remains of me but bones, still they will proclaim, 'Lord, who is like unto Thee?'"

And suddenly, Noah felt his own soul come back into himself.

"I can do this thing," he whispered.

The old man smiled again and nodded. "If you do this thing for me, I promise that God will save you. The day will come when you will not be in this place. You will be alive because you have done this thing."

Noah felt his soul stretch into his body, felt it reach to his fingertips, to his toes. He felt it fill him.

The old man walked calmly into the gas chambers. He held the *talis koten* tightly.

Later, when the crying had stopped and the gas had cleared from the chambers, Noah took the body of the old man from the contorted crowd and laid it gently on the ground. He pried his fingers from the *talis koten* and smoothed it out, straightening the fringes. Then, lifting the man onto his lap, Noah drew the *talis koten* over the old man's head and tied it along his sides. He held his cheek against the old man's, and his soul whispered,

"Speak to the children of Israel, and tell them to make themselves a tassel on the corners of their clothes in every generation. Thus will you remember and do all of my commandments, and so be holy before your God."

Then, gently, gently, Noah carried him to the cart.

. . .

At the end of thirty days, all those who had worked at the gas chambers stepped into them themselves. Except Noah. He was sent back to his barracks, and will still be there when the camp is liberated.

"Make Yourselves Ready"

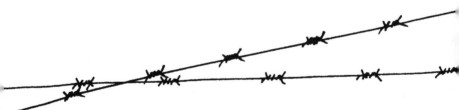

*A*nd then the night comes when the guards follow the women into the barracks. "There will be a selection tomorrow." They smile. "Make yourselves ready."

But there is nothing to do to make themselves ready, and that night they gather around Mara as they have always done, only this time they are all surprised by the beauteous glow of Mara's face. And they all know, as if God Himself has told them, that this night will be the last night of Mara's stories. They hunch together and hold hands as Mara reaches out for a child, and then another child, and another and another until all the children of the barracks sit upon and around her.

And still her face glows. It glows brighter and brighter until it seems as if it is a benediction upon them all.

And she tells them her last story.

Remember!

Once upon a time, the King of a prosperous and happy people stood out under the stars. Suddenly, who knows how, he understood something terrible: The next autumn's harvest would make everyone who ate from it mad. The King shook with the unbearable knowledge. If his people ate from the harvest, they would be insane. If they did not, they would die of starvation.

For a moment—just a moment—he thought of a solution for himself. He would gather all of the last harvest that remained, and he would eat it through the next year. He at least would not go mad.

But the sudden hope chilled him. What of the children of his kingdom? What of those he honored most deeply? What of those who had been most faithful to him for years beyond memory? And what of his own most dearly beloved?

As he came back in from under the stars, he had decided. He was a King and would always be a King. If his people were to fall into madness, then he as their King would follow them there.

But he was not yet done.

In the morning, he called his closest friend, Moshe, to him, and told him what he knew. Moshe stood in silence before his King but trembled for his friend.

"Moshe," said the King, "you shall build a granary. And you shall fill it with what remains of the last harvest. And you alone shall have the key to enter the granary."

"Yes," said Moshe, still trembling.

"When all my people, and when their King, will eat of the next harvest, you alone shall eat from the granary."

Moshe said nothing. He was weeping.

"When all my people, and when their King, will fall into madness, you alone will have escaped the curse."

"And what shall I do then?" asked Moshe. "What shall I do without my King and without my people?"

"You shall be a witness," explained the King. "You shall go all over the land, from farm to farm, from town to town, from street to street, from house to house and room to room, and you shall tell our story to all who will listen. You shall tell them, 'I will say dark sayings about days of old, sayings that will not be hidden, sayings that must be told from one generation to the next, so that each generation to come may know them.'"

Moshe bowed his head.

"You shall say, 'Once there was a people,' and you shall shout it far and wide, with all your might, with all your strength. You shall shout, 'Once there was a people. Remember! Remember! Remember!'"

Notes to the Stories

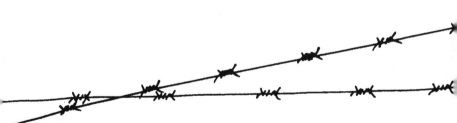

The Violinist and the Master

I first heard this tale when I was a child; it was told to me by a friend who came from a family of musicians. The story came from his father, who had heard it from his father. My friend told it as a tale of absolute and pure self-sacrifice, which, of course, it is.

The tale as he told it had a protagonist with no name, and that was important to the notion of its selflessness. The sacrifice came from someone whose name would never be known, given as a gift. But in this version, I have given him the name of Salek after Salek Bot, a young Jewish partisan who was killed in Paris, 1942, while making a bomb to attack a German barracks.

His hands had not been trained for war. He was a violinist.

The Dark of the Earth

Rabbi Zusia and Rabbi Elimelekh were two of the great Hasidic figures of the late 1700s; the daughter of a rabbi would have heard many tales of them. The stories about the brothers reflect an enormous sensitivity to the world around them; Zusia in particular was known as someone keenly aware of the power and presence of suffering.

Though Rabbi Zusia and Rabbi Elimelekh came to the town of Auschwitz one hundred and fifty years before the earth would actually be darkened with terrible and murderous barbarism, they felt it coming. What came was one of the most notorious of the death camps, through which hundreds of thousands passed. It was a place where souls survived only three to four months; sometimes eight thousand people were gassed to death each day. It remains, and will always remain, one of the darkest places on earth.

The stories of the two rabbis upon which this story is loosely based are told by Elie Wiesel in his *Souls on Fire: Portraits and Legends of Hasidic Masters* (New York: Random House, 1972): 115–116.

A Globe

This bittersweet story, a joke really, has been retold in a number of places, most recently in Steve Zeitlin's *Because God Loves Stories: An Anthology of Jewish Storytelling* (New York: Simon & Schuster, 1997): 224. Most versions have the final question asked by the father: "Pardon me, have you anything else to offer?" he inquires after looking over all the countries of the globe in S. Felix Mendelsohn's version (*Let Laughter Ring* [Philadelphia: Jewish Publication Society of America, 1941]: 135–136). But in this version, I changed the ending so that it is asked by a child eager to find a way to help his father. The story thus loses some of its dark humor, perhaps, but gains in its poignancy. It is a judgment on the terrible injustice of the world's refusal to pay attention to what was happening in Nazi Germany.

Rabbi Weizmann and Chaim are named after Chaim Weizmann, the Zionist leader who in the late 1930s foresaw the destruction of Europe's Jews and fought to find a way to help emigration out of Europe to Palestine.

The Spilled Soup

This tale is adapted from a story about Rabbi Elimelekh of Lizensk, in Poland. In that tale, the Emperor of Austria is to issue a new edict with which he had planned to terrorize the Jews of his country. Only the Rabbi and his disciple Mendel are perceptive enough to understand what has happened in this tale, a tale that is full of hope, since it demonstrates the power of a single holy man. At the same time, the spilled ink remains only a temporary solution to the terrible laws designed to destroy the Jewish communities in any land that the German army occupied. The laws proclaimed against the people of Lizensk in this version of the story are only a small portion of actual laws that the Nazis enforced, laws that eventually led to total identification and then separation of Jewish families.

The earlier version of Rabbi Elimelekh's tale is found in Martin Buber's *Tales of the Hasidim, Vol. 1: The Early Masters* (New York: Schocken, 1947): 259.

The Reply

I have here adapted one of the stories of Rabbi Shneur Zalman of Ladi, in northern Russia, who died in 1813, having believed all his life that the sparks of God are inherent in all things, all creatures. In his version, he has been imprisoned in St. Petersburg, and the inquisitor is the chief of police. The chief is moved at the Rabbi's reply and shouts, "Bravo!" But his heart trembles. In my version, the officer trembles as well, but in front of the crowd, he cannot, will not acknowledge what he knows to be a just and truthful reply.

The Rabbi's refusal to flee is modeled on Rabbi Baruch Safrin of Komarner, who, when urged to escape the coming terror, refused and said, "I am with them in their distress."

Rabbi Shneur Zalman's tale may be found in Martin Buber's *Tales of the Hasidim, Vol. 1: The Early Masters:* 268–269. The Rabbi's concluding prayer is from the *Amidah,* this version from Lawrence A. Hoffman's *My People's Prayer Book: Traditional Prayers, Modern Commentaries, Vol. 2:*

The Amidah (Woodstock, Vt.: Jewish Lights Publishing, 1998): 57. The original of the lintel that has the slashed words "Know Before Whom You Stand" is in the United States Holocaust Memorial Museum in Washington, D.C., in the exhibit of *Kristallnacht.*

The Pretzel Bakers

This well-known tale is one of the humorous folktales of the Holocaust; some versions have an elderly Jewish man, rather than a Rabbi, suggest that it is all the fault of the bicycle riders, rather than the pretzel bakers. Despite the horror of the time, the story creates humor through the besting of the SS officer. The besting of the stronger by the weaker is a motif that also informs many of the humorous folktales that come out of slavery times in America.

The prayer of the Rabbi is the *"Birkat Kohanim,"* "The Priestly Blessing," here reprinted from Lawrence A. Hoffman's *My People's Prayer Book: Traditional Prayers, Modern Commentaries,*

Vol. 2: The Amidah (Woodstock, Vt.: Jewish Lights Publishing, 1998): 42.

The terrible poignancy of the Rabbi's final question—the question that wins back the confidence of the young boy—comes out of that question's familiarity. It is a question that has been asked in every century, but never with more urgency than during the Holocaust.

A Calf Is a Calf

Trickster stories, common in cultures around the world, are usually tales of a clever but powerless trickster overcoming the will and authority of someone much more powerful. That is the situation in this tale, which is here adapted from a story by Rabbi Menahem Mendel of Rymanov, Poland, who died in 1815. In his tale, it is the lord of the manor who cheats a peasant and boxes him on the ears; the peasant then takes his clever revenge on the lord. Rabbi Mendel would tell the tale on the night of the seder, and it is his commentary that I follow when Mara names the calf "Israel." Rabbi

Mendel also names the lord, or the officer in this version: Sammael, the name for Satan. But I chose to leave the officer nameless for the reason that Mara gives.

In Rabbi Mendel's story, the peasant beats the lord three times as his vengeance, until the lord finally acknowledges his cheating. I have imagined that Mara would have seen enough beatings, however, and feel that she would have no desire to include a beating in her stories for the children of the barracks. So in this version, Michael cheats the officer by selling him animals for much more than they are worth—an appropriate punishment for what the officer did to him in the market.

Rabbi Mendel's version of the story may be found in Martin Buber's *Tales of the Hasidim, Vol. 2: The Later Masters* (New York: Schocken, 1948): 132–134.

The Unexpected Treasure

"The Unexpected Treasure" is adapted from a tale about Rabbi Eisik, who was born in Kraków.

When the Rabbi found the treasure, he used it to build a House of Prayer for his community. Here young Eisik uses it to help his poor family escape Poland.

Unfortunately, the last dream would probably not have come true for Eisik. The money that he discovered could have been used to bribe the police and those ministry officials who controlled emigration. And the desperate need for Jewish families to escape led to high bribes indeed. But even so, after 1939, it was almost impossible for a Jewish family to immigrate to America, though until that time only one fifth of the immigration quota—the number of immigrants from a single nation or ethnic group—had been filled. The Western nations' refusal to change immigration policies doomed hundreds of thousands, if not millions.

The story of Rabbi Eisik is told in Martin Buber's *Tales of the Hasidim, Vol. 2: The Later Masters:* 245–246; and by Jiri Langer in "Reb Eisik's Treasure," in *The Jewish Spirit: A Celebration in*

Stories and Art, edited by Ellen Frankel (New York: Stewart, Tabori & Chang, 1997): 201–203.

The Dance

The most important source that I draw upon for this story is a tale of the Baal Shem Tov and his wife, who is worried that his disciples will drink up all the wine and leave none for the sabbath meal. But there are numerous Hasidic tales that attest to the sacredness of dance and music as an expression of spiritual joy that affect the story. A tale by the mid-nineteenth-century Rabbi Israel of Rizhyn, for example, tells of the Rabbi ordering music to be played during a time of fasting. During the Holocaust, it was said that the Spinker Rebbe, Rabbi Yitzchak Isaac Weiss, danced on the train on the way to the death camp at Auschwitz. In my version, Rabbi Haim is named after the Dombrover Rabbi, Haim Yehiel Rubin, who led his disciples in a great dance just before they were murdered and buried in graves they themselves had dug.

The exhortation toward trust and faith in this tale comes from a teaching of the Baal Shem Tov, and the power of that trust and faith is suggested by having the Rabbi's wife unbolt the door at the end of the tale.

The story of the dance and the sabbath meal is found in Martin Buber, *Tales of the Hasidim, Vol. 1: The Early Masters:* 52–53, as is the teaching of the Baal Shem Tov (60). The tale of Rabbi Israel is found in Martin Buber's *Tales of the Hasidim, Vol. 2: The Later Masters:* 55.

From the Stones

The destruction of Jewish cemeteries, particularly in Poland, was one more way that the Nazis tried to obliterate the European Jewish culture, yet another desecration. For this story, I have set that desecration against the vision of Rabbi Hananiah ben Teradyon, who was martyred in ancient Rome under Emperor Hadrian. Burned at the stake, the Rabbi called to his daughter that the words on the Torah that had been mockingly wrapped around him were flying into the air; only the parchment was burning. His story is celebrated yearly in the Musaf prayer for Yom Kippur—he is one of ten martyrs so celebrated. The text for that story may be found in the liturgical prayer books, as well as in David G. Roskies' anthology of Jewish responses to catastrophe, *The Literature of Destruction* (Philadelphia: Jewish Publication Society, 1988): 47.

The Three Men

The Belzer Rabbi's spectacular escape from Belz in Galicia, in southeastern Poland, occurred between 1943 and 1944 and finally ended in Budapest. It was an escape that sparked many tales. In the version of this story told by a Hasidic narrator to Jerome R. Mintz for his *The Legends of the Hasidim: An Introduction to Hasidic Culture and Oral Tradition in the New World* (Chicago: University of Chicago Press, 1968): 367, the tale is quite short, only seven sentences. It is also quite ambiguous; it recounts two miracles: the beclouded car that keeps the Belzer Rabbi safe, and the three men who suddenly and unexpectedly allow the car to pass when it is being challenged. But it is not clear in that version who the three men are. Are they Nazis who simply fouled up their search for the Rabbi? Or is there another explanation?

I have chosen to heighten the scale of the biblical echoes, linking the three men to those biblical messengers from God who appeared, for example, to Abraham to announce the miraculous conception of his son Isaac, or to Lot to bring him out of Sodom before its destruction. In stories such as these, the messengers—always unidentified—are clearly from God, and so their presence in this version seems consonant with the miraculous cloud.

The question of why this Rabbi was saved while so many others perished is one that not even the angels, perhaps, can answer.

Which Shoebox?

Abraham is here named for the biblical Abraham, who also was ready to leave at a moment's notice.

The story is based on a tale told in a lecture entitled "Stories as Equipment for Living," by Barbara Myerhoff and recorded in Thomas R. Cole, David D. Van Tassel, and Robert Kasenbaum, eds., *Handbook of the Humanities and Aging* (New York: Springer Publishing, 1992). My version has some changes in the contents of the two boxes to heighten their stark differences, and the ending has been shifted: In Myerhoff's version, Abraham takes the second box, but I prefer to let the reader decide which box Abraham would think would be the right one to keep.

The story is set during *Kristallnacht,* the Night of Broken Glass, on November 9, 1938, when so much of the wanton, destructive persecution of the Jewish people in Germany began in earnest.

Shards

I have left this story unresolved, as it is in the version by Rabbi Israel of Rizhyn, who died in the middle of the nineteenth century. Will Shmulik betray the Rabbi or not? Here I have made the betrayal much worse than in Rabbi Israel's version: There, the servant Shmulik betrayed the Rabbi by allowing himself to be bribed so that the Rabbi might be spied upon while he prayed; in this version, Shmulik has betrayed a whole people.

Rabbi Israel's version is told in Martin Buber's *Tales of the Hasidim, Vol. 2: The Later Masters:* 65. His city of Rizhyn is in Russia.

God in Court

There is a kind of terror in this story, in that it overturns all expectations of a loving God. I have taken it from the stories of Rabbi Elimelekh, who placed it in Austria and framed it with a threatening edict against the Jews. Because of the suit and Feivel's success, Rabbi Elimelekh has God cause the Emperor to cancel the edict that he has planned. But I have left out this happier ending in my adaptation, and leave the justice of the accusation hanging. Here I have followed the tradition of Rabbi Mordechai of Chernobyl, who died in 1837. Rabbi Mordechai accused God of violating his own commandments in not adequately preserving and protecting the people of Israel.

The version by Rabbi Elimelekh is found in Martin Buber's *Tales of the Hasidim, Vol. 1: The Early Masters:* 258–259.

The Tsaddik, *One Righteous Soul*

This is a tale that sounds as if it might come from the biblical book of Judges in its sense of providential answer to prayer, a prayer that saves an entire nation. The question, of course, is this: Who is the *tsaddik* who stops Rommel? Is it the Rabbi who maintains the traditions of prayer and praise even as the world around him seems to panic into chaos, or is it the Or ha-Haim, a *tsaddik* in his own right, who honors the prayers being said at his grave? On a deeper level, the story suggests what a single righteous man might do in the face of what seems to be insurmountable, unstoppable evil.

This is an adaptation from the tale of a Hasidic narrator in Jerome R. Mintz's *The Legends of the Hasidim:* 367–368. There, the story is told of the

Hushatener Rabbi; I have left the Rabbi anonymous so that he may stand for all the righteous souls who prayed for providential help during the Holocaust.

The "Good Morning"

This tale is based loosely on one told by storyteller and writer Steve Sanfield; it is also told in Yaffa Eliach's *Hasidic Tales of the Holocaust* (New York: Oxford University Press, 1982): 109–110. It is a story that questions how apparently ordinary people—like Herr Mueller—could become a part of something so vastly evil. It is a question with no answer.

I was tempted here to change the story's ending and have Herr Mueller motion to the left, as it is almost impossible to imagine someone in such a position having any sense of humanity or compassion left that would lead him to grant Herr Shaul even a chance at life. But I let the ending stand in the perhaps vain hope that in some camp, at some moment, at least one man responsible for sheer evil felt the beginning of shame.

Herr Shaul is named after Rabbi Shaul, who as a young boy traveled with the Baal Shem Tov and met another young boy, Ivan, with whom he danced. Many years later, when Rabbi Shaul was a scholar, he was stopped by robbers, taken from his coach, and brought to their leader, who instantly recognized the Rabbi as his boyhood friend. Ivan commanded his men to return Rabbi Shaul's money and take him back to his coach. That story is told in Martin Buber's *Tales of the Hasidim, Vol. 1: The Early Masters:* 43–44.

The Wonder

I have compiled this tale from several Hasidic stories, creating a story that mirrors the traditional tales of a Jewish soul who has lost his faith confronting the soul of one who has maintained his own, even in the midst of the Holocaust horror. A number of tales conflate this confrontation of faith

141

(which is almost impossible to understand) with the loss of faith (which is almost impossible not to understand).

The *kapos* were criminals, often murderers, given authority over the prisoners beneath them; their cruelty was often beyond that of the guards, the cruelty of the powerful over the powerless. The story of the wonder itself—the lack of response from the powerful—is actually told with regard to a guard rather than a *kapo* in the version by the Bobover Rabbi recorded in Jerome R. Mintz's *The Legends of the Hasidim*: 365.

I have given the boy the name Chaim after the phrase "L'Chaim," "To Life." The Rabbi's comment about God in hiding is drawn from the stories of Rabbi Pinhas of Korets, who died in 1791 and believed that one should love the evil-doer all the more to make up for the lack of love that the evil has caused in the world. His tale is told in Martin Buber's *Tales of the Hasidim, Vol. 2: The Later Masters*: 122.

The Rod

Another humorous folktale from the Holocaust, where this time Hitler himself is bested. In some versions, Hitler, who was superstitious, holds a séance to speak to the spirit of Moses, who tells him that the rod is in the British Museum in London. In another version, Hitler has died and calls across from hell to Moses to find out how he crossed the Red Sea. Both of these versions are told in Steve Lipman's *Laughter in Hell: The Use of Humor During the Holocaust* (Northvale, N.J.: Jason Aronson, Inc., 1991): 83, 138–139. S. Felix Mendelsohn, in his *Let Laughter Ring* (Philadelphia: Jewish Publication Society of America, 1941): 142, tells yet another version, in which Hitler orders a replica of Michelangelo's statue of Moses stolen from the Louvre, the museum in Paris, and brought back to his office in Berlin, where he prays to it, asking Moses how he crossed the sea.

The version here is loosely based on Sam Levenson's retelling of the folktale, a version he taped in a

1976 interview for the William E. Wiener Oral History Library of the American Jewish Committee, now held in the Jewish Division of the New York Public Library. A transcript of Levenson's oral version of the story is reprinted in Steve Zeitlin's *Because God Loves Stories*: 223.

I have heightened the distinction between Hitler and the Rabbi by suggesting their very different responses to the beauty of the scene on the coast of France. Hitler's response is one of frustrated acquisition; the Rabbi's response is one of praise to God.

Keep Tight Hold

This story is based loosely on one told to Yaffa Eliach by Rabbi Israel Spira and published in Eliach's *Hasidic Tales of the Holocaust*: 3–4 as "Hovering Above the Pit." Eliach's work is the most important collection of Holocaust narratives told in the tradition of the Hasidic tale; that work is complemented by her monumental *There Once Was a World: A 900-Year Chronicle of the Shtetl of*

Eishyshok (Boston: Little, Brown, 1998). In Eliach's telling of Rabbi Spira's tale, the protagonists are a rabbi and a man who has lost his faith. The guards tell their prisoners that they must jump over a pit; those who fail will be machine-gunned to death. The pit is impossibly wide, and no one can jump it until the Rabbi leaps. When he opens his eyes, he finds himself on the far side, along with the man who has lost his faith. The man asks the rabbi how he made such a jump, and the Rabbi explains that he made it by holding on to his ancestors, to the law and Torah, and to God. "But how did you make it?" he asks the man. "By holding on to you" is the reply.

Here the tale of faith and courage is seen from the vantage point of a father and son, and suggests a continuing resource of hope even in the midst of hell itself. It is set in the Janowski Road Camp in eastern Poland, where 200,000 people were murdered in much the same way that the tale describes.

The story of the Baal Shem Tov takes place during his youth, as he is chased to the Dniester River.

It is recorded in Martin Buber, *Tales of the Hasidim, Vol. 1: The Early Masters:* 74.

The Miracle

Rabbi Israel ben Eliezer, the Baal Shem Tov, was the founder of the mystical Hasidic movement in the eighteenth century; his stories are told by Elie Wiesel in his *Souls on Fire:* 34–35, 37. They are stories, Wiesel writes, of joy and hope, but that does not necessarily make them happy stories.

In this remarkable tale, the miracle comes not from the Rabbi, but instead from those who have been murdered, their bodies thrown into the pit. Astonishingly, they do not demand that they be made alive again; they ask for no miracles. Instead, they give thanks for the witness of the Baal Shem Tov's other miracles. That witness is more important to them than their own lives.

Of this story, Wiesel writes, "And so, in the kingdom of Hasidic legend, the Baal Shem follows his disciples to the end of night. Another miracle?

Certainly not. Death negates miracles, the death of one million children negates more than miracles."

And yet we live, remembering, hoping, grateful for the witness.

The Promise of the Talis Koten

This story comes out of Auschwitz and has been told by several tellers, including a survivor who narrated the version on which this telling is loosely based. This teller's version may be found in Jerome R. Mintz's *The Legends of the Hasidim:* 366–367.

I have given the boy the name Noah for its biblical association; I have not named the old man, so that he may stand for all who held on to their beliefs and traditions when it might have seemed that such holding was impossible. The old man's response to Noah's question of faith is quoted from the Piazesner Rabbi, Kalonymos Kalmish Shapiro, whose writings were hidden away in the Warsaw Ghetto after his death and later found and published in Israel as *Holy Fire.*

The prayer is from the *Sh'ma* ("Hear, O Israel"), the section from the Book of Numbers, chapter 15, that deals with the tassels on the prayer shawls. This version is from Lawrence A. Hoffman's *My People's Prayer Book: Traditional Prayers, Modern Commentaries, Vol. 1: The Sh'ma and Its Blessings* (Woodstock, Vt.: Jewish Lights Publishing, 1997): 85.

Remember!

This tale is retold from a story by Rabbi Nahman of Bratzlav, recorded by Elie Wiesel in his *Souls on Fire*: 202. Rabbi Nahman's stories are strange, unsettling tales of dreams and visions, as is this one, told by him at the beginning of the nineteenth century. But it is prophetic also; it foretells one of the most important lessons of the Holocaust: to remember always. In my version, Moshe is named after Moshe Flinker, who was arrested in Brussels and died in Auschwitz in 1944. He was seventeen. In his diary he wrote, "We are witnesses. . . . We were brought into being by an inferno of suffering; and we are a sign of peace to you." His story is told in *We Are Witnesses,* edited by Jacob Boas (New York: Henry Holt, 1995): 80–113.

The King's final admonition is based on Psalm 78: 2–6. It is the same passage that opens the first collection of Hasidic tales, written by Rabbi Dob Baer ben Samuel in 1814: *Shivhei ha-Besht, In Praise of the Baal Shem Tov,* now available translated and edited by Dan Ben-Amos and Jerome R. Mintz (Northvale, N.J.: Jason Aronson, Inc. 1993).

GO**FISH**

GARY SCHMIDT

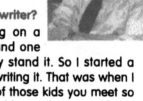

What did you want to be when you grew up?
I wanted to go into the navy. Then I wanted to become
a vet. Sometimes, I still want to become a vet.

When did you realize you wanted to be a writer?
Not until graduate school. I was working on a
dissertation, and a lot of it was in Latin; and one
night I was so sick of it that I could hardly stand it. So I started a
children's book, and it stunk, but I enjoyed writing it. That was when I
was about twenty-six or so. I was not one of those kids you meet so
often who know they want to be writers and have poems and keep
journals, and work for the school newspaper.

What's your first childhood memory?
A spider that a kid drew in kindergarten. Somehow, whenever I think
of my first memory, that's it. The kid's name was Glen Sweiteck, and
our teacher, Mrs. Hershey, hung the picture on the wall. I remember
being frightened by it because it was so scary. That was my first
encounter with art.

What's your most embarrassing childhood memory?
Probably throwing a gallon of bright yellow oil paint on my brother. It
was impossible to get out, and it was in his hair and everywhere.

As a young person, who did you look up to most?
Probably my grandmother. Her name was Gertrude Smith. She was
an amazing reader, a wonderful storyteller, and a very calm and

pacific person. I went to the library first with her. She got me an adult library card when I was ten.

What was your worst subject in school?

When I was young, reading was my worst subject. We were divided into groups very early on and, though they gave us innocuous names, I was in the pumpkin group, and knew that was the worst. We were always 2-3 books behind the best readers—and we were constantly reminded of that. Later, a teacher named Ms. Kabikoff made me read, and introduced me to a lot of wonderful books. I read some books that were too easy for me, but she let me read them, and that gave me the confidence to try older books. If it weren't for her, I probably wouldn't be a reader. And no one can be a writer who isn't a reader first.

What was your first job?

I washed dishes for a Presbyterian church; it was $6 an evening. After that, I worked up at a camp, also washing dishes, landscaping, cleaning pools. I hated cleaning pools.

How did you celebrate publishing your first book?

I remember I was doing advising days, getting a student every fifteen minutes, and in the middle of that, Virginia called. I said, "Hey, Virginia, what's up?" thinking it was a student. And then I realized who it was, and I said, "Is this 'the' Virginia Buckley?" and she said, "This is 'a' Virginia Buckley." But we didn't really celebrate.

Where do you write your books?

We have a small outbuilding, outside the house, one of the early buildings on the farm we live on. The roof was falling in when we moved in and, since the house was built in 1837, we decided we would use tools from only that period to rebuild it. The books and my desk are there; it's heated with an old, wood-burning stove. I type on a 1953 Royal typewriter.

Where do you find inspiration for your writing?

I'm always a little leery of the word inspiration because it seems to suggest that an idea comes from on high and hovers above like a muse. I think the word I'd rather use is "awake." I think all writers need to be awake to the moments that you feel will lead to a story. When you come upon that idea, you recognize it as a potential story—which sounds easier than it is.

Which of your characters is most like you?
I think on some level, they all are. In *First Boy*, I think that Cole is a lot like me. In *The Wednesday Wars*, Holling is closest to my own experience. In *Lizzy Bright and the Buckminster Boy*, Turner is the kid I would have ideally liked to have been. Cole is living the way I would have liked to live, on a farm with tractors.

When you finish a book, who reads it first?
My wife, Anne. But she doesn't read it until it's completely finished, and we don't even talk about it until it's completely finished. I think if you talk about a book, you diffuse the energy of writing it. You're in the process of discovery as you write; if you talk it through, all of it is gone. You've worked it out, expressed it. That's why I'm not a part of a writers' group.

Are you a morning person or a night owl?
Definitely morning. At 9:00 PM, I'm in bed.

What's your idea of the best meal ever?
Any meal that ends with my wife's apple pie. It really doesn't matter what comes before.

Which do you like better: cats or dogs?
Dogs. No human being really likes cats. People just say they do because they feel sorry for them. Cats can't like anyone because they're so arrogant. You always know what a dog's thinking, what they're about to do. There's something generous about a dog.

What do you value most in your friends?
Loyalty, hard work, a shared commitment to a redemption of the culture.

Where do you go for peace and quiet?
Home.

What makes you laugh out loud?

Really good writing, a clever handling of language. It comes so rarely, and hardly ever comes in the media, but when it comes, it's perfect. There used to be a show called *Brooklyn Bridge* by Gary Goldberg about kids growing up in the 1950s, one family was Jewish, the other Roman Catholic. The guy from the first family falls in love with Mary in the second family, and all of the situations arise from those complications. I loved it. *The West Wing* is also brilliantly done.

What's your favorite song?

Beethoven's Ninth Symphony.

Who is your favorite fictional character?

The one that pops to mind is Oliver from *Oliver Twist*. I think he's a brilliant character by Dickens. Also the warden in Anthony Trollope's books. He's a sweet, sweet guy, the archetypal vision of sweet. But if I had to pick just one, I'd go with Oliver Twist.

What are you most afraid of?

A fear that something ill might happen to my children.

What time of the year do you like best?

Winter. To walk outside when the moon is out after a freshly fallen snow, there is nothing like it. Or after the first frost when the sun is coming up.

What is your favorite TV show?

I don't watch any now. It's too depressing. And now with the notion of DVDs, you can watch without being interrupted every eight minutes.

If you were stranded on a desert island, who would you want for company?

My wife.

If you could travel in time, where would you go?

Revolutionary Boston. I would like to have seen that. Can you imagine it? The beginning of a new country.

What's the best advice you have ever received about writing?

Eighth grade, Mr. Shamsky, "Show, don't tell." It's a cliché now, and you hear it in every single writing class, but that was the first time I'd heard it. I can even hear his voice as he spoke it and wrote it on the board.

What do you want readers to remember about your books?

That they're about hope. That they're about the notion that goodness is important and honor is important and nobility of purpose—all those are important. That it's important to grow up and not be lulled into a culture that says stay an adolescent because you're the best consumer when you're an adolescent. Turn your faces toward adulthood. You see commercials of four guys in their forties, sitting together drinking beer and watching the Super Bowl—and that's a good time? I'm thinking you act like that when you're twelve. It's a good time, but it's a time designed to end.

What would you do if you ever stopped writing?

I won't.

What do you like best about yourself?

I think I can be disciplined, and I think writing is all about discipline. It's not about waiting for inspiration or the muses or waiting to be an auteur. It's about sitting at your desk and getting your 2,000 words out.

What is your worst habit?

You probably should ask my wife that.

What do you consider to be your greatest accomplishment?

My six children.

What do you wish you could do better?

My six children.

What would your readers be most surprised to learn about you?

Probably that I write on a typewriter. In this day and age, where it's just assumed that you work on a computer, writing on a typewriter with a ribbon seems like something out of the Stone Age.

Made in the USA
San Bernardino, CA
18 May 2020